**HO**

CW01395764

presented by HOM

# Going Out Out
## by Barney Norris

*Going Out Out* opened at HOME, Manchester, on 16 October 2025

# Going Out Out by Barney Norris

CAST

**Ian**   James Quinn
**Raz**   Darren Kuppan
**Lauren**   Verity Henry


CREATIVE TEAM

**Director**   Jess Edwards
**Sound Designer/Composer and Co-Arranger**
   Duramaney Kamara
**Lighting Designer**   Adam Foley
**Music Director and Co-Arranger**   Jordan Paul Clarke
**Set and Costume Designer**   Miriam Nabarro
**Casting Director**   Jane Anderson

# Biographies

### James Quinn | Ian

James comes to HOME for *Going Out Out*, having appeared numerous times at the venue's celebrated forerunner, Manchester's Library Theatre. James has appeared in UK theatres including the Royal Exchange, Sheffield Crucible, the Old Vic, Birmingham Rep, Coventry Belgrade, Oldham Coliseum, Leicester Haymarket, Bolton Octagon and Greenwich Theatre.

TV and screen work includes *Brassic, After the Flood, Queen Charlotte: A Bridgerton Story, Peacock, Early Doors, Doctor Who, Father Brown, Bancroft, Gentleman Jack, Pennyworth, Safe, Coronation Street, Fat Friends* and the film *Apostasy*.

James has performed in dozens of BBC radio dramas and comedies including his own comedy series, *Sir Ralph Stanza's Letter from Salford*. Other writing includes *Twenty-20* (Stephen Joseph Theatre), and his time as writer-in-residence at HMP Manchester (Strangeways).

James co-founded *JB Shorts*, Manchester's award-winning festival of new short plays. His short, *At the End of the Day*, became BBC Radio 5 Live's first drama commission. James is also matchday commentator at FCUM TV and Radio.

### Darren Kuppan | Raz

TV credits are *Dodger* (NBC Universal/BBC), *Home From Home, Spooks* (BBC), *Coronation Street, Britannia High, Emmerdale, The Adam & Shelly Show* (ITV).

Theatre credits include *Mahabharata* (Canada & America tour/Barbican, London), *The Jungle Book* (Theatre by the Lake), *Around the World in 80 Days* (Octagon Theatre), *Let the Right One In* (Royal Exchange Theatre), *The Card* (Claybody Theatre), *Merry Wives of Windsor, Pride and Prejudice* and *The Jungle Book* (Grosvenor Park Open Air Theatre/Storyhouse), *Around the World in 80 Days, Hamlet, A Christmas Carol, Europe,* and *Road* (Leeds Playhouse), *Under Three Moons* (Box of Tricks Theatre), *Hard Times* (Northern Broadsides), *Guards at the Taj* (Bush Theatre), *Partition* and *Bollywood Jane* (West Yorkshire Playhouse/BBC Radio Leeds), *The Tempest* and *Cymbeline* (The Globe), *East is East* (Birmingham Rep), *An August Bank Holiday Lark* (Northern Broadsides), *Duck* (Z-Arts), *England Street* (Oxford Playhouse), *Melody Loses Her Mojo* (20 Stories High), *Much Ado About Nothing* (RSC), *We Love You City* revival (Belgrade/Talking Birds), *Great Expectations* (ETT/Watford Palace), *A Christmas Carol* (Library Theatre), *Rafta Rafta* (Octagon/New Vic), *We Love You City* (Belgrade/Talking Birds), *Aladdin* (Theatre Royal Stratford East), *Jamaica House* (The Dukes) and *Arabian Nights* (New Vic).

**Verity Henry | Lauren**

Theatre includes *JB Shorts, Wuthering Heights At Hurricane Speed, A Great War, Touched, At The End of The Day* (Real Life Theatre Company); *The Possibility of Colour, Classic* (Hope Mill Theatre); *Hard Times* (Oldham Coliseum); *War Stories* (Breath Out); *Don Quijote* (contentedorafflicted HOME); *Dumbheads* (Goofus); *Blind Date* (Jermyn Street Theatre/Biteback Productions/Bolton Octagon Theatre); *Hard Times, Getting Married, A Doll's House* (The Library Theatre Company).

Television and film includes *Football Fantastics, Meet The Richardsons, Hijack, Hullraisers, Coronation Street, Wolfe, Ted's Top Ten, Cold Feet, Hollyoaks, The A Word, Outing, Leatherbird, 3 In A Bed, Drifters, The GateKeeper, Hebburn, Doctors, Coronation Street, A Touch of Frost, Confessions, Heartbeat.*

**Jess Edwards | Director**

Jess Edwards is an award-winning director, dramaturg and writer represented by Curtis Brown. Recent directing includes: *Elephant* (Menier Chocolate Factory) by Anoushka Lucas, *Conversations After Sex* (Park Theatre) by Mark O'Halloran, *War & Culture* (New Diorama) by Nina Segal, *Albatross* (Playground Theatre) by Isley Lynn, *Hotter* (Soho Theatre) and *Fitter* (Soho Theatre).

As director, Jess's work won *The Stage* Debut Award for best playwright (*Elephant*, 2023) and the MTR Best New Musical Award (*Sparks*, 2018). She has recently completed an attachment at the National Theatre.

As writer, her debut play *Private View* was shortlisted for the Women's Prize and the Yale Drama Series Prize and is currently in pre-production. Her debut screenplay *Clitorati* won the Studio21 Drama Script Award and is currently in development with 5Acts. She is under commission from Kindred Partners writing a new book musical.

**Barney Norris | Writer**

Barney Norris's work has received awards from the International Theatre Institute, the Critics' Circle, the Evening Standard, the South Bank Sky Arts Times Breakthrough Awards and the Royal Society of Literature, among others, and been translated into ten languages.

His plays include *Visitors* (Up In Arms, Arcola, Bush and tour), *Every You Every Me* (Salisbury Playhouse), *Eventide* (Up In Arms, Arcola and tour), *Echo's End* (Salisbury Playhouse), *While We're Here* (Up In Arms, Bush, Farnham Maltings, BBC Radio 4 and tour), *Want* (National Theatre Connections), *Nightfall* (Bridge Theatre), *Song and Dance* (BBC Radio 4), adaptations of Ishiguro's *The Remains of the Day* (Out of Joint, Royal & Derngate and tour) and Lorca's *Blood Wedding* (Up In Arms and Wiltshire Creative), *The Queen of the Isle of Wight* (BBC Radio 4), *The Wellspring* (Royal & Derngate and tour), *We Started To Sing* (Arcola Theatre), *The Band Back Together* (Farnham Maltings, Arcola Theatre and tour) and an adaptation of David Foenkinos' *Second Best* (Riverside Studios).

His novels are *Five Rivers Met On A Wooded Plain*, *Turning For Home*, *The Vanishing Hours* and *Undercurrent*. He has also published two books of non-fiction, *To Bodies Gone: The Theatre of Peter Gill*, and a book about his father, *The Wellspring: Conversations with David Owen Norris*.

He is a lecturer in creative writing at the University of Oxford, reviews fiction regularly for the *Guardian* and has previously sat on the Writers Guild theatre negotiating committee and the Society of Authors sustainability committee, as well as chairing their scriptwriters committee. In 2024 he stood for the Green Party in Salisbury at the General Election. From 2010–2020 he was co-artistic director of the touring theatre company Up In Arms, where, as well as his own plays, he produced landmark revivals of Robert Holman and David Storey.

## Duramaney Kamara | Sound Designer/Composer and Co-Arranger

Duramaney Kamara is a multidisciplinary sound designer and composer. Under the pseudonym 'D L K', he is also a recording artist and producer who releases music under his indie label Be Free 888 Repertoire.

Theatre credits include: *Bangers* (Arcola/Soho/Edinburgh Fringe); *Wolves on Road* (Bush); *Barcelona* (West End); *Grow Up*, *C3 Stories* (Company Three); *Mantelpeace* (Young Vic Taking Part); *Swim Aunty, Swim* (Belgrade, Coventry); *Love Steps* (Omnibus/Wrested Veil); *Cinderella* (Brixton House); *Clyde's* (Donmar Warehouse); *August in England, House of Ife, Project 2036* (Bush); *Suckerpunch* (Queen's, Hornchurch); *Bootycandy* (Gate, Camden); *Anansi the Spider* (Unicorn/ Regent's Park Open Air); *Christmas in the Sunshine* (Unicorn); *Moreno, Roman Candle* (Theatre 503); *Collection* (Tara Arts); *The Death of a Black Man, Hoes* (Hampstead); *The Dark* (Fuel/Ovalhouse); *Living Newspaper* editions 4 & 5, *Dismantle This Room, My Mum's a Twat, Instructions for Correct Assembly, katzenmusik* (Royal Court).

## Adam Foley | Lighting Designer

Theatre credits include: *A Christmas Carol* (Derby Theatre); *These Majestic Creatures* (The SJT); *Pop Music, The Culture*, and *Our Mutual Friend* (Hull Truck Theatre); *Haywire, A Role to Die For, Some Mothers Do 'Ave' Em, I'm Sorry Prime Minister I Can't Quite Remember*, and *Around the World in 80 Days* (The Barn); *The Wedding Party* (Oldham Coliseum); *Sanctuary, Taxi, My Voice Was Heard But It Was Ignored* and *Smile Club* (Red Ladder); *Small Wonders* (Punchdrunk); *The Jungle Book* (The Dukes); *Patient Soldier* (Storytime & Seven Dials Theatre); *To the Moon and Back* (Concrete Youth); *Sh!t Life Crisis, Dead Girls Rising, The Golden Fleece, A Super Happy Story (About Feeling Super Sad), Pig*, and *Small Plans* (Silent Uproar); *The Merry Wives* (Northern Broadsides); *We Used To Be Closer Than This, Robin Hood, The Little Mermaid, Cinderella, Aladdin* and *Dick Whittington* (Middle Child); *Sleeping Beauty* and *Aladdin* (CAST); *John Proctor is the Villain* (Leeds Conservatoire) and *Imaam Imraan* (NYT).

**Jordan Paul Clarke | Music Director and Co-Arranger**

Jordan Paul Clarke is an award-winning writer, composer, musical director and improviser.

He's a musical director of Olivier Award-wnning *Showstopper: The Improvised Musical* ('incredible . . .defies belief', *Telegraph*) and has toured with multi-award-winning Mischief Theatre (Olivier-nominated *Mischief Movie Night*). Other MD Credits include *Broken Wings* (Assistant MD, Dubai Opera House), *AIDS Baby* (Barbican), *Animal Farm* (National Youth Theatre), *Ride* (Garrick Theatre), *Cinderella* (Newbury Corn Exchange) and music supervisor of British Youth Music Theatre.

As writer and composer, original musicals include: *Happy* at Waterloo Vaults and the Kings Head ('profound, modern theatre at its best', *Boyz*), *Building Paulus* (UK tour), *Friday Night Sinner* at Soho Theatre ('would do Mel Brooks proud', *Chortle*; 'flawless music', *Musical Theatre Review*) and *Angry Salmon* at Theatre Royal Plymouth ('is it really all about salmon?', Claude-Michel Schönberg) and, currently in development, *Raising Gays*.

With writing partnership 'Forristal and Clarke': *P.S. I'm a Terrible Person* (currently in development, shortlisted for the Charlie Hartill Award, Pleasance Theatre, and the Stiles and Drewe Mentorship Award 2021), and *Public Domain* (Vaudeville Theatre) (***** *Everything Theatre*; ***** *GScene*; 'Pick of the Week', *The Times* Hotlist 2021); featured on BBC RADIO 2 ('innovative', *Telegraph*; 'original and edgy', *Guardian*), for which they were nominated for *The Stage* Debut Awards 2022 for best composer, lyricist and book writer.

**Miriam Nabarro | Set and Costume Designer**

Miriam is an Australian/British UK based scenographer, theatre designer, facilitator and visual artist. She is Creative Associate with 20 Stories High, shows regularly with Tin Man Arts and has worked extensively internationally as a humanitarian, artist and activist.

Theatre credits include: *Stars* (Tamasha Theatre/Brixton House/ICA/UK tour); *Lucky Tonight* (Home/Traverse); *Please Do Not Touch* (China Plate/Belgrade Theatre); *K56, Small Forward, King Staakhs Last Hunt, Dogs Of Europe* (specialist design work, Belarus Free Theatre/Barbican/US tour); *Jane Eyre* (GSMD); *High Times, Dirty Monsters* (20 Stories High/Graeae); *At the Forest Edge* (RSC); *Catch, I Am a Theatre, Sweatbox* (Clean Break); *Bone Sparrow* (Pilot Theatre); *Aaliyah After Antigone* (Freedom Studios); *I Told My Mum I Was Going on an RE Trip, Touchy, Buttercup* (20 Stories High/BBC); *The Little Price* (Fuel/EIF); *Processions* (Artichoke/Clean Break); *The Welcoming Party* (Theatre-Rites/ MIF); *Broke N Beat Collective* (20 Stories High/Ruhr Festival); *The Great Game, Afghanistan* (Tricyle Theatre/US tour), *Palace Of The End* (Royal Exchange/ Traverse/Amnesty Freedom of Speech Award), *War Correspondents* (Abbey Theatre); *Bang Bang Bang* (Royal Court); *Cupboard of Delights* (National Theatre).

### Jane Anderson | Casting Director

Jane Anderson has cast BAFTA Award-winning productions. Her career began in production before moving into casting in 2004. She has cast extensively for screen, and more recently began casting for stage.

Stage credits include: *Kinky Boots* (Chester Storyhouse), *The Clothes They Stood Up In* (Nottingham Playhouse), *Alice In Wonderland* (HOME Manchester), *The Walk – The Sleeping Child* (MIF21).

Screen credits include: *The Ancestors* (BBC Film/RedBag Pictures), *Lagging* Series 1 (CBBC), *Creeped Out* (CBBC/Netflix), *Viking Destiny* (Fatal Black/ Misfits Entertainment), *Bucket* (BBC/Company TV), *Spying on Hitler's Army: The Secret Recordings* (Channel 4/October Films), *Hard Boiled Sweets* (Fatal Black/ ContentFilm International) and BAFTA Cymru-winning *Convenience* (Urban Way).

Having grown up in an English and Jamaican household in London, travelled extensively and then lived overseas in her 20s, she relocated to the North West in 2014. She continues to work between there and London.

She is passionate about fair representation within the industry, and as she has extensively cast young performers, is keen to give support and opportunities to many starting out in the industry. This led her to becoming an Industry Associate at LAMDA drama school, where she supports and offers guidance to their graduates, alongside her casting work.


### Karl Sydow | Producer

Karl is producing the 2026 international tour of Sting's *The Last Ship* with a new book by Barney Norris. Karl produced *The Last Ship* at the Ahmanson in LA and the Golden Gate in San Francisco (2020) and at the Princess of Wales, Toronto (2019), following a UK and Irish tour (2018). Current productions include a US tour of *AVA: The Secret Conversations*, starring Elizabeth McGovern. Karl is also building a new theatre in London. Recent productions include: *The Unfriend* by Steven Moffat (Criterion and Wyndhams), UK tour of *Spike* by Ian Hislop and Nick Newman, and *Dirty Dancing: The Classic Story On Stage* (Dominion Theatre), which he has produced around the world since 2004.

In North America, he has produced Broadway productions of *The Seagull* and *American Buffalo*, *Backbeat* (Royal Alexandra, Toronto; Ahmanson, LA), and international tours including *The Last Confession* with David Suchet, and *Our Country's Good* (the original Tony-nominated production).

Other recent theatre includes: *Blood Wedding* by Barney Norris; *An Hour and a Half Late* (Theatre Royal Bath and UK tour); *Noises Off* (Lyric Hammersmith and Garrick, West End); *The Light in the Piazza* (Royal Festival Hall / LA Opera / Lyric Opera of Chicago); *Toast* (West End / UK tour); *Sweat* (Gielgud, West End – *Evening Standard* Award for Best Play); *Valued Friends* (Rose Theatre, Kingston); *Invisible Cities* with 59 Productions (MIF / Brisbane Festival, Australia); Alan Ayckbourn's *The Divide* (Old Vic and EIF); David Hare's *The Moderate Soprano* (Duke of York's); and *Sketching* by James Graham (Wilton's Music Hall), as well as the films *Red Joan* and *Unicorns*.

# HOME

HOME is Manchester's premier arts centre and a registered charity, welcoming over 7 million visitors since opening. HOME features two theatres, five cinemas, an art gallery, and a popular restaurant. HOME collaborates with artists from both the UK and around the world to produce and present exceptional visual art, cinema, and theatre experiences. Placing a strong focus on UK theatre, international works, new commissions, and artist development, HOME is deeply rooted in the community, pushing creative boundaries, embracing experimentation, and sharing bold, exciting art with as wide an audience as possible. Our patrons include director Danny Boyle, actress Suranne Jones, playwright and poet Jackie Kay CBE, and artist Rosa Barba.

homemcr.org | Instagram @HOMEmcr
Twitter @HOME_mcr | Facebook HOMEmcr

FUNDED BY

MANCHESTER CITY COUNCIL | ARTS COUNCIL ENGLAND | GMCA | THE NATIONAL LOTTERY

FOUNDING SUPPORTERS

Weightmans | Garfield Weston | The Granada Foundation | THE OGLESBY CHARITABLE TRUST | Transport for Greater Manchester | University of Salford MANCHESTER | MANCHESTER SCHOOL OF ART

Did you know that HOME is a charity? We need your support to bring the best film, theatre and art to Manchester and inspire the next generation. Get involved at www.homemcr.org/support

# Going Out Out

Barney Norris's work has received recognition and acclaim from, among others, the International Theatre Institute, the Critics' Circle, the *Evening Standard*, the Society of Authors, and the South Bank Sky Arts Times Breakthrough Awards, and been translated into nine languages. His plays include *Visitors*, *Eventide*, *Nightfall*, *The Wellspring*, *We Started to Sing*, *The Band Back Together*, and adaptations of Ishiguro's *The Remains of the Day* and *Second Best* by David Foenkinos; his novels include *Undercurrent* and *Five Rivers Met on a Wooded Plain*.

BARNEY NORRIS

# Going Out Out

faber

First published in 2025
by Faber and Faber Limited
The Bindery, 51 Hatton Garden
London, EC1N 8HN

Typeset by Brighton Gray
Printed and bound in the UK by CPI Group (Ltd), Croydon CR0 4YY

A CIP record for this book
is available from the British Library

ISBN 978-0-571-40220-5

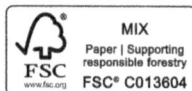

MIX
Paper | Supporting
responsible forestry
FSC
www.fsc.org
FSC® C013604

Printed and bound in the UK on FSC® certified paper in line with our continuing
commitment to ethical business practices, sustainability and the environment.
**For further information see faber.co.uk/environmental-policy**

Our authorised representative in the EU for product safety is
Easy Access System Europe, Mustamäe tee 50, 10621 Tallinn, Estonia
gpsr.requests@easproject.com

2 4 6 8 10 9 7 5 3 1

Going Out Out, presented by HOME and Karl Sydow,
opened at HOME, Manchester, on 16 October 2025, with
the following cast:

**Ian** James Quinn
**Raz** Darren Kuppan
**Lauren** Verity Henry

*Director* Jess Edwards
*Sound Designer/Composer and Co-Arranger*
    Duramaney Kamara
*Lighting Designer* Adam Foley
*Music Director and Co-Arranger* Jordan Paul Clarke
*Set and Costume Designer* Miriam Nabarro
*Casting Director* Jane Anderson

For Pegleg

# Characters

**Ian**
sixty, a man from Manchester

**Raz**
about thirty, a man from Manchester

**Lauren**
thirties, Ian's daughter

*Setting*

Act One is set in a house in Manchester.

Act Two is set in a Manchester working men's club.

.

GOING OUT OUT

# Act One

*Lights up on a back garden in a Manchester suburb. Ian is holding a watering can and wearing a dress. He sings along to the radio as he waters the garden. Raz enters. Ian doesn't see him. He has a bag of shopping in each hand. Ian starts to get into his singing a bit more. When he sees Raz, he stops abruptly.*

**Raz**  All right, Ian?

**Ian**  Oh.

**Raz**  It's Raz.

**Ian**  Raz?

**Raz**  I was ringing the bell but no answer, so I thought I'd just come round the back.

**Ian**  As the actress said to the bishop.

**Raz**  Sorry?

**Ian**  Nothing. What do you want?

**Raz**  I've brought your shopping.

**Ian**  *(dawning realisation)* Oh. Raz! Sorry, I've caught up now. I didn't recognise your voice with your face there too. Lots to take in! That's my things. You've brought my things round.

**Raz**  That's it.

**Ian**  Thank you. Thank you very much.

**Raz**  I thought you might be out. When I was ringing. So I was just gonna leave it by the back door, I put a note through the front.

**Ian** Quick thinking. I was just doing the garden. Hot this year.

**Raz** Yeah.

**Ian** Keeps getting hotter. That's Isambard Kingdom Brunel's done that.

**Raz** Is it?

**Ian** He invented the engine.

**Raz** Did he?

**Ian** I think so. Or something like that. I wasn't out.

**Raz** I know that now.

**Ian** Course, yeah. You can see me.

**Raz** Anyway. Here's your stuff. I'll just put it here, shall I? And don't worry about the note on the mat, that's about this, yeah? That's all solved now.

**Ian** You're talking to me like I'm special.

**Raz** Special?

**Ian** You know.

**Raz** We don't say that now, mate.

**Ian** No?

**Raz** But I didn't mean to talk to you weird.

**Ian** There's nothing wrong with me.

**Raz** Great. That's great, then.

**Ian** Well I don't mean there's *nothing* wrong with me. I just mean I'm not. You know.

**Raz** Differently abled.

**Ian** You what?

**Raz** Don't worry.

**Ian**  Look, do you want to stop and have a brew?

**Raz**  Yeah?

**Ian**  What?

**Raz**  No, it's just. You've never invited us in before. I've never even seen you till now, have I.

**Ian**  No, that's right.

**Raz**  I thought you didn't like people.

**Ian**  Sorry?

**Raz**  That's what they said to me. In my head I actually always imagined you surrounded by horses. At the end of *Gulliver's Travels*, right, the book, yeah, he decides he's had enough of people, and he only talks to horses and that's his lot. So when they said you kept yourself to yourself I actually laughed at the time, cos the image came to me of a man in an armchair and in the next armchair, this horse sitting looking at him. And neither of you talking.

*Beat.*

**Ian**  Who told you that?

**Raz**  That you didn't like people?

**Ian**  Yeah.

**Raz**  Well, the guys at the hub.

**Ian**  The hub?

**Raz**  The matchmakers.

**Ian**  The matchmakers?

**Raz**  Sorry, I'm not being specific enough, am I.

**Ian**  They're all just words to me.

**Raz**  I mean the charity that set us both up.

**Ian**  Oh. I see.

**Raz** They said you'd only wanna talk through the door as you weren't comfortable meeting new people.

**Ian** That's right.

**Raz** But we only just met and you've asked me in for tea.

**Ian** Well, look. Raz. Raz?

**Raz** Yeah.

**Ian** I'll be totally honest. I'm worried you might report me.

**Raz** Report you?

**Ian** That's right.

**Raz** For what?

**Ian** For being able to walk and that.

**Raz** You think I'd report you for being able to walk?

**Ian** If I'm not actually eligible, like. I didn't mean to say there was nothing wrong.

**Raz** If you're not actually eligible for what?

**Ian** For my shopping.

**Raz** It's not just for wheelchair users, is that what you mean?

**Ian** Is it not?

**Raz** It's whoever needs it. All kinds of needs. They'll have assessed you and decided.

**Ian** Have they?

**Raz** I mean they must have done or I wouldn't be here, would I.

**Ian** That was that phonecall, maybe. Not you and me. That patronising woman, you know? I suppose you don't know. You weren't there.

**Raz**  Did they ask you questions about yourself?

**Ian**  That's it. And I told them about how I can't do bloody online shopping cos I don't know computers. I haven't even got one. It's only on my phone and my thumbs are too big so I don't use it. When I try and do things on my phone I just cry. Is that why they let you do my shopping?

**Raz**  Yeah. I guess so.

**Ian**  And you reckon I'm eligible?

**Raz**  I reckon so, yeah.

**Ian**  Honestly, that's such a relief. I'm very lucky you do my shopping.

**Raz**  It's a pleasure. I'm glad to help.

**Ian**  Did they not have any Phish Food?

**Raz**  Fish food?

**Ian**  My ice cream.

**Raz**  Oh. Yeah, I've got it.

**Ian**  Were you just gonna leave it by the back door?

**Raz**  Well, yeah, I suppose I was.

**Ian**  In this heat?

**Raz**  Well I thought you were out. I couldn't think what else to do.

**Ian**  Glad you caught me then.

*Raz puts his bags down.*

**Raz**  They still don't have those eye drops.

**Ian**  Do they not?

**Raz**  I asked. I went in two places.

**Ian**  I appreciate that.

**Raz** They have these different ones but not the brand you ask for.

**Ian** Honestly, this country. Nothing's kept stocked up.

**Raz** Yeah, right.

**Ian** I was a lorry driver.

**Raz** Were you?

**Ian** As a younger man. I didn't stick at it. Never at home. So once we had the kids. I hated that job. After Michael was born I went and worked on the trains and that was better.

**Raz** Did you sleep in your cab?

**Ian** What?

**Raz** When you used to drive a lorry.

**Ian** I had a little bunk.

**Raz** I always wondered what those were like.

**Ian** Why?

**Raz** Sorry?

**Ian** Why did you wonder that?

**Raz** I've never seen one.

**Ian** There's nothing worth seeing.

**Raz** Fair enough.

**Ian** The worst was the washing. I got through a great deal of wet wipes. Kath was always having a go.

**Raz** What for?

**Ian** She'd buy 'em for the babies and I'd nick 'em for work.

**Raz** Was Kath your wife?

**Ian** That's right. This is hers, actually. This dress I'm wearing.

**Raz** Oh right.

**Ian** You won't tell anyone about that will you?

**Raz** Course not, Ian. Why would I do that?

**Ian** Oh, come off it.

**Raz** Honestly mate, I'd be the last person with a problem with that.

**Ian** Yeah?

**Raz** Absolutely. No judgement. You're all right.

**Ian** I'm not gay.

**Raz** Okay.

**Ian** You are.

**Raz** I am.

**Ian** Should I not have said that?

**Raz** It's fine. In the circumstances it feels sort of relevant, I guess. And I'm not ashamed, so –

**Ian** Seriously?

**Raz** Sorry?

**Ian** You don't feel shame?

**Raz** Excuse me?

**Ian** I feel shame all the time.

**Raz** Oh. I thought you were saying something else.

**Ian** I felt shame ever since I was a boy. I remember running down a beach with my top off to my mother, and some bloke laughed at me because I was all jiggling. And my mam saw him and didn't say anything, as if it was understandable, you know? As if it was natural to laugh at me. I remember that being when it got in. I felt shame because I bought my clothes too tight for me, to try and be less fat than I am, and then the tightness of my clothes made me feel fatter. I felt shame because I was too wide on buses and aeroplanes, and the people next to me had to shuffle up. I felt shame because I sweated too much, and I thought that must make me smell, and I tried to deodorise, but now and then, you know? I felt shame because my thighs rubbed together and I'd get all rashes in the summer. I felt shame because my wife and children loved me. And I knew I didn't deserve that.

**Raz** Bloody hell, Ian.

**Ian** Sorry. Oh dear. I took the handbrake off and rolled down the hill.

**Raz** You did a bit.

**Ian** Now I'm in the bad thoughts and the weeds.

**Raz** Well put yourself back into gear maybe.

**Ian** I didn't mean to.

**Raz** It's all right.

**Ian** It's cos I'm on my own most of the time. This feeling like there's a dam. You know, like so much wanting out?

**Raz** Like when you've eaten a whole tub of Phish Food.

**Ian** Well yes, actually.

**Raz** You're not fat, mate.

**Ian** That's what everyone says. I know better. I used to say I know I'm anorexic cos every time I look in the mirror I see a fat bloke staring back at me! But then my daughter had a run-in with bulimia, so I wouldn't tell that joke now in public.

**Raz** I probably wouldn't, yeah.

**Ian** I read in the paper about people getting cancelled. I don't want any of that.

**Raz** I think you've more or less cancelled yourself already.

**Ian** Have I?

**Raz** In that you've withdrawn from the world.

**Ian** Is that all it is? I thought it was worse than that.

**Raz** Tell you what I always say. If you go into life pure of heart then most of the time you'll be all right. If you're not prejudiced, and you say sorry when you get things wrong, people are generally quite understanding.

**Ian** I'm not prejudiced against anyone.

**Raz** Glad to hear it.

**Ian** Comes with being a union man. Anyone taking part in the struggle is part of the struggle, know what I mean?

**Raz** I do, yeah.

**Ian** I'm just glad I haven't had to deal with it.

**Raz** Deal with what?

**Ian** Far as I can tell, being gay's a fucking nightmare. Or at least it used to be in my day. I don't know as much about it now. But the coming-out stuff. The homophobia. Wasn't even legal when I was really young. Being gay, not homophobia. Homophobia was popular as Christmas. I just think it sounds like a headache.

**Raz** I don't know. It's love, Ian, it's brilliant.

**Ian** You wait.

**Raz** How d'you mean?

**Ian** You're still young. You wait forty years. I'd say come back and tell me then how brilliant love is, but I won't be here to hear it, will I.

**Raz** Bloody hell, mate, there's bees in your head, ent there.

**Ian** Yeah, there are, yeah.

**Raz** What happened?

**Ian** My wife died.

**Raz** I see.

**Ian** When she was ill I took early retirement, so I could look after her. But that meant I got used to being at home. And it was just me and her you know? An island kingdom. And once she was gone I couldn't quite leave the island. I still go out now and then. Couple of doctor's appointments. My kids visit. I bloody hate that.

**Raz** Yeah.

**Ian** Oh, it's agony. You got kids?

**Raz** No.

**Ian** It's a trap. Don't do it. I still jump when I see mine, I forget where I am, I expect them to be little. Time slips when you're on your own. On an average day I basically live in the summer of eighty-six.

**Raz** Why then?

**Ian** When?

**Raz** The summer of eighty-six.

**Ian** Summer I met Kath. I think the moment all of us emerge into the world becomes very important for ever after. That time sort of sets around you like a jelly. So you can see all the things that have gone on since, but you only really see 'em through the world you first got used to. Everything afterwards is coloured by that. Sorry.

**Raz** What?

**Ian** I'm talking too much.

**Raz** I should go.

**Ian** I can make us a brew, if you'd like?

**Raz** No, it's fine. I'm meeting someone anyway.

**Ian** Out for a pint?

**Raz** That's it.

**Ian** Just imagine.

**Raz** Do you think you'll do that again some day?

**Ian** Is it pathetic? I suppose it sounds pathetic. I'd just had enough life, know what I mean? I don't have room for any more, but I can't bring myself to put an end to it, and anyway Kath told me I mustn't, said it would affect the kids. So I thought, I'll just put a lid on. Have what I've got and no more, thank you. Everyone worries how they come across, don't they.

**Raz** Do you have someone to talk to about all this?

**Ian** About what?

**Raz** Well it sounds like you're struggling.

**Ian** What good's talking about all that?

**Raz** No, sure. Well, I'd better leave you to it. Okay if I leave this here?

*He gestures to the bags on the ground.*

**Ian** Fine, yeah.

**Raz** All right. I'll see you then. Good to meet you.

**Ian** And you. Nice to put a face to the name.

**Raz** See you later.

**Ian** Yeah. All right.

*Raz leaves. Ian puts down the watering can, and buries his face in his hands, and sobs. Then he stops and goes to the bags. He takes out the tub of Phish Food. Takes the lid off. It's melted. He starts to drink it. Lauren, Ian's daughter, comes out of the house.*

**Lauren** There was a note on the mat saying – Dad.

**Ian** Oh. Lauren.

**Lauren** What the fuck are you doing?

**Ian** Well, it was melted.

**Lauren** I don't mean that. Is that Mum's? Dad, what the fuck?

**Ian** I was missing her, darling. I was missing your mum.

*Lights change. Raz performs a song in half-drag.*

2

*Ian's house. Raz and Ian. Both have cups of tea. Ian is dressed in his own clothes.*

**Raz** Honestly Ian I'm so bloody sorry. I just thought about the last time we spoke, and I think I took some liberties when I called them, I said it was all a bit more urgent than it was, I never thought they'd go kicking the door in though. I felt terrible once you weren't there.

**Ian** It's fine.

**Raz** It's not fine, I got your front door busted by the police.

**Ian** They fixed it up though.

**Raz** Oh, you don't know the half of it. That was me sorted that. When they'd been right through the place and you weren't here, they said I was lucky I didn't get booked for wasting police time, and then they were about to leave, and I said, what about his door you've kicked in? His house isn't secure, you can't leave it like that! And they said yeah, the door wants fixing, but we don't do that, that's homeowner. And I said, the homeowner isn't here. He's missing. You just told me he's missing. That's the whole point. So they said, well, are you his family? And I said no, but he has got family, I just don't know who they are. And they said well, but you know him, don't you? So could you fix his fucking door? So I called a locksmith and they had like, an emergency service, and they came out and they got it fixed.

**Ian** So *you* fixed my door?

**Raz** Well no, the locksmith. I was here while it happened.

**Ian** I didn't know.

**Raz** Did you find the key all right? I didn't know where to leave it when he finished.

**Ian** Yeah, fine.

**Raz** I was stuck for a while on that. Thought I'd have to stay till you came back. And I didn't know when that'd be, cos you were missing, and I started spiralling, I was like, how long would I be willing to wait? Would I have to just live here, what if you'd gone for ever? Then I thought, he'll have a key for the back door. So that's when I left the note on the front and the new key on the table and hoped you'd be able to work it out.

**Ian** Did you pay for it?

**Raz** It's all paid for, yeah.

**Ian** I should cover that.

**Raz** Don't be daft, I made 'em kick it in.

**Ian** Are you sure?

**Raz** It was my fault, Ian.

**Ian** Only I'm not flush, as you can see.

**Raz** Honestly, it should be me.

**Ian** Well, I appreciate it.

**Raz** So where were you? I was still worried. I still thought you might have gone off a bridge. I got the police to file a missing person's. Actually I should probably get that cancelled.

**Ian** Will they have my poster up? Am I on milk cartons?

**Raz** I don't know what happens.

**Ian** Might be interesting to let it run and see. See how many people recognise my face if it's up on billboards or whatever.

**Raz** Only they've already bollocked me about wasting police time, so I might get in trouble if I don't phone in that you're back at home.

**Ian** That's true.

**Raz** I'll call 'em. So where were you?

**Ian** I got sectioned, actually.

**Raz** Come again?

**Ian** Bit of a turn-up for the books.

**Raz** In a hospital? *Sectioned* sectioned?

**Ian** Yeah, the full Monty.

**Raz** Bloody hell.

**Ian** But they let me back, so it's fine.

**Raz** Do you mind if I ask what happened?

**Ian** Well, it was actually my daughter told 'em to do it.

**Raz** Why'd she do that?

**Ian** She thought I was mental. Should I not say 'mental' any more?

**Raz** Not ideally, no, Ian.

**Ian** What was the phrase you used? 'Differently abled'?

**Raz** That doesn't exactly apply here either.

**Ian**  It was because I was wearing the dress.

**Raz**  Yeah?

**Ian**  She turned up right after you did, actually. Let herself in, I forgot she was coming. She found your note on the mat. Then she came out into the garden, took one look at me, thought I was. You know.

**Raz**  And they just believed her?

**Ian**  Well there was a bit more to it. After we talked, me and her, not me and you, I became quite distressed. And when I'm distressed, I have this bad habit. I sort of hit myself in the head.

**Raz**  Okay.

**Ian**  I have this brick I keep in the garden. Holds a tarp down over the barbecue. When I get stressed I go and get it. Then I hit myself in the head.

**Raz**  Bloody hell.

**Ian**  I know it's stupid. I don't have full control of it.

**Raz**  You can't be doing things like that.

**Ian**  Then I go to hospital, and say, hello, I'm afraid I've hit myself in the head with a brick again, could you be a darling and check me out? It's played havoc with my health insurance premium. I'm joking. Obviously I don't have health insurance.

**Raz**  Ian, I don't want you to do this.

**Ian**  Well, that's kind.

**Raz**  No, but Ian you mustn't.

**Ian**  Like I say, I'm not in full control of it. But anyway, Lauren got upset, and that upset me, so I did that.

**Raz**  While she was there?

**Ian** I waited till she left. That'd be awful to do it in front of her. But then she came back, and she found me, so she called them.

**Raz** And they thought that was worth a cheeky little sectioning.

**Ian** That's it, yeah. And fair enough, I say.

**Raz** You're not wrong Ian, you don't wanna do that.

**Ian** I know. I think it'll help in the moment.

**Raz** Keep a tally of how often it does.

**Ian** Never.

**Raz** That's the point I'm making.

**Ian** They drove me down to the hospital, kept me under observation for three days. Nice people. They let me go, obviously. They can tell there's nothing wrong with me.

**Raz** Well.

**Ian** Not big wrong.

**Raz** Well.

**Ian** They let me go, anyway. Told me I had a bit of a concussion, and might experience insomnia and mood swings for six months. I said what's new, I already have 'em. They said in that case you ought to stop hitting yourself in the head. I had to get back home on the bus. I could hardly stand it. All those people. Then my front door key wasn't working. Then I read your note and got in. You were lucky a burglar didn't read it. Then they could have known I was out.

**Raz** I didn't think of that.

**Ian** I think you're more or less safe round here. Good neighbourhood.

**Raz** Yeah.

**Ian** And I'm one of the more feared gangsters in Salford.

**Raz** Are you?

**Ian** No, course not.

**Raz** Have you spoken to your daughter since you got home?

**Ian** Funnily enough, I haven't prioritised that.

**Raz** Pissed off?

**Ian** First few days I was fuming. I get that I hit my head with a brick. But that's not why she called the hospital. She called the hospital because of the dress. And I knew it was a weird thing to do, like. I wasn't about to walk down the street. But it makes me feel close to her. Makes me feel like she's almost here. And I like something loose fitting for the garden on a hot day.

**Raz** Sure.

**Ian** I know it's weird but I dunno what's wrong with it.

**Raz** Nothing. It's not weird.

**Ian** That's what I think! But she doesn't. And that upsets me.

**Raz** Would Kath have minded?

**Ian** She'd have told me I was being soppy, mooning over her.

**Raz** It will have been shock as much as anything else.

**Ian** With Lauren?

**Raz** Yeah.

**Ian** I hope so. I was surprised, I must say. In my day there used to be loads of cross-dressing, nothing very weird about it. Kath and I used to watch it at the club. Stand-up acts, you know? And a bit of singing. And Danny La Rue and Lily Savage on TV. We thought it was funny. Maybe Lauren didn't know about that.

**Raz** It's a big thing now, still.

**Ian** Yeah?

**Raz** Do you watch much telly?

**Ian** It's my only significant relationship.

**Raz** Do you know *Drag Race* then?

**Ian** Oh yeah, I've seen that. I didn't like it. It's very different to what I used to go to. Much more American. And high fashion. Different songs. But everything's more American these days. You can't tell because you're young, but it's a big thing.

**Raz** It's gayer too, maybe.

**Ian** England?

**Raz** I meant *Drag Race*.

**Ian** Oh right.

**Raz** I do drag.

**Ian** Do you really?

**Raz** I do the clubs round Manchester, yeah.

**Ian** Fucking hell. How amazing. The bloke who does my shopping. Anyone could be anyone, know what I mean? How come you got into it?

**Raz** Freedom, really. The freedom of a mask. Breaking out of people's expectations of what someone ought to be like if they look like me.

**Ian** You any good?

**Raz** I think I'm all right.

**Ian** Would you get on the telly?

**Raz** I dunno if I'd try.

**Ian** Why not?

**Raz** If you believe in it, I don't know how you can. Drag is punk. It's against all normativity. Drag's about attacking expectations. You can't do that and do TV.

**Ian** Selling out.

**Raz** That's it. People misunderstand. People think it's men dressed as women. It's not. It's a space for attacking assumptions. Radical philosophy in suspenders. You can't do RuPaul and believe in that. RuPaul's the McDonald's of drag, know what I mean? We all end up there late at night now and then, but we're none of us proud of it the following morning.

**Ian** I'll tell you what would piss me off about it. If I had to do drag on the telly. They make everyone do this backstory thing. You know, everyone has to be terribly damaged? And they talk to the camera and say their dad rejected them, or they cry about their mums, and I think it's invasive, really. All of them being made to talk about pain they've had to recover from in public.

**Raz** Yeah, hate that.

**Ian** Right?

**Raz** Invasive.

**Ian** Hey, Raz?

**Raz** You're not gonna ask me what traumatic event pushed me into drag performance are you, Ian?

**Ian** No, I was wondering, can you do a death-drop? Everyone seems very proud of that when they do 'em on the TV, but I can't tell if it's actually difficult.

**Raz** Honestly, it's really not. Look.

*Raz gets up and death-drops.*

Not much to it.

**Ian**  Do you reckon I could learn?

**Raz**  I think it's essential you never try.

**Ian**  I'd do my back probably.

**Raz**  You'd fracture half your body.

**Ian**  I was only wondering.

**Raz**  Next life maybe.

**Ian**  Oh, don't. I think that all the time these days. Didn't used to.

**Raz**  I think it's like the football season. You know how when the season starts, none of the players are really fit yet, no one gets stressed if they lose a game or two. And then in January everyone sits up. Suddenly they start counting down. And the last five games, there's this mad pressure on 'em.

**Ian**  Squeaky bum time.

**Raz**  Squeaky bum time. But they're worth the same three points as the games back in August. It's just that no one was counting then.

**Ian**  That's a very good simile that, Raz. I'm not quite sure what for, but I like it.

**Raz**  Well it's for life.

**Ian**  Yeah?

**Raz**  We all waste the first half. Then we spend the second half listening for the final whistle.

**Ian**  Oh. Well isn't that fucking depressing. Do you want another brew?

**Raz**  I ought to be off really.

**Ian**  Do you have someone to get back home to?

**Raz**  I live with my mum. Just for now. I'm gonna move on.

**Ian**  Are you?

**Raz**  I was thinking of going abroad, yeah.

**Ian**  Abroad?

**Raz**  I don't know where. I just thought, not England. Have you ever had a mate who goes off the rails, like? And they get into coke or they're with the wrong partner. And you try and talk to them but they won't listen. And there comes a point where you say, I'll have to leave this. Just for a bit, till they pull it together. Cos every time I see them they're being a twat.

**Ian**  That's England?

**Raz**  That's England. It's not worth the bother. I thought I might give it five years and see if she breaks up with her toxic boyfriend, or whatever it is that's England's fucking trouble.

**Ian**  When you going?

**Raz**  Few months maybe. Once I've saved the money.

**Ian**  That soon?

**Raz**  'Fraid so. I'm sure you'll miss me.

**Ian**  Well, I'll miss you doing my shopping.

**Raz**  You never know, you might feel up to it by then. Looks like you've got back into talking to strangers.

**Ian**  Tell you what, Raz. I feel we're getting on. Do you feel we're getting on all right?

**Raz**  Sure.

**Ian**  Well that's good. I'm glad to hear that. And you know how you made the police kick my door in? And could therefore be said to sort of owe me?

**Raz**  Where's this going, Ian?

**Ian** Well, you've got me thinking of Lauren.

**Raz** Okay.

**Ian** I suppose I ought to try and see her. Do you think you'd be up for being here when I did?

**Raz** Oh.

**Ian** Not to mediate, exactly, just to keep it on the level. Keep me from getting too upset. I'm sorry to ask, maybe it's inappropriate. I know we don't really know each other. But I'm feeling not too anxious talking to you, and I thought maybe if you had the time to spare, like –

**Raz** The only thing I'd question, Ian, is whether I'm the best person to ask. Cos when your daughter saw you in a dress, she got you sectioned. So is bringing a drag queen the next time you meet her just a little bit confrontational?

**Ian** I hadn't thought of that.

**Raz** I'm not saying I wouldn't, I just wonder. Not that I'd be dressed up or anything. But I hope you know what I mean.

**Ian** No, I hadn't thought of that. The trouble is that there isn't anyone. If I try and think of who to ask, there isn't anyone springs to mind. And I was never much good with Lauren, like. I was never much good as a father. Kath was better at talking to them. Lauren and her brother.

**Raz** You don't talk as much about your son.

**Ian** He doesn't talk as much to me.

**Raz** Fair enough.

**Ian** Maybe it was daft to ask you. Sorry, mate. Forget about it.

**Raz** No, I wasn't saying I wouldn't. If you can't think who else could be there, I'd be happy to come along.

34

**Ian**  Would you?

**Raz**  Just to make the tea, like. I don't know anything, I won't stick my nose in.

**Ian**  Do you think it would seem like ganging up?

**Raz**  I can't answer that, you'll know better.

**Ian**  Maybe I should sleep on it.

**Raz**  Sure. But I'm game if it'd help you.

**Ian**  Thanks, mate.

**Raz**  No worries. I'll be off now, though. Dinner with Mother.

**Ian**  I hope you also sometimes hang out with people your own age.

**Raz**  Don't you worry about me. I'll show myself out. And give me a ring about that in the morning.

**Ian**  All right.

**Raz**  See you then.

**Ian**  See you later.

*Raz sings a number as the scene changes.*

*Lauren and Ian in Ian's living room.*

**Lauren** Hiya Dad.

**Ian** Hello love. Come here.

**Lauren** You all right?

*He hugs her. Raz enters.*

Raz?

**Raz** Bloody hell.

**Lauren** What are you doing here?

**Ian** Do you know each other?

**Raz** Are you Ian's –

**Lauren** Raz works down the club.

**Raz** Is Lauren your daughter?

**Ian** Well, how small the world. You know I said I'd like to have a friend here? Well, this is him. He gets my shopping.

**Raz** How are you?

**Lauren** Bit thrown, to be honest.

**Ian** It's fate maybe. You want a brew?

**Lauren** Sorry?

**Ian** It's fresh. Hang on. I'll get it.

*Ian goes to the kitchen to get Lauren a cup of tea.*

**Lauren** I was wondering who it was gonna be. He called me and said he'd like a friend here, and I didn't have a problem with that, but Dad doesn't have any friends, you know? He hasn't made a new friend since 1992. So I was expecting his mates from the pub, or else I thought maybe he was getting cuckooed. But that's not you, is it.

**Raz** You know it isn't.

**Lauren** Yeah, sure, course I do. I was just checking. So you do the shopping?

*Ian enters with tea, gives it to Lauren.*

**Raz** That's it. You know he's signed up to a charity sets things up like that for people who don't find it easy to go out?

**Lauren** I signed him up to that.

**Raz** Right.

**Lauren** I do his shopping sometimes too. Whenever I can.

**Ian** She does.

**Raz** That's great. But when you don't, that's me who goes and does it.

**Lauren** Why did you get involved with that?

**Raz** I had spare time and I wanted to be useful.

**Lauren** Right.

**Raz** What?

**Lauren** No, that's good of you. That's all there is to it?

**Raz** What else would it be?

**Lauren** It's not some form of community service?

**Ian** Lauren.

**Lauren** I'm sorry, I just wanted to ask.

**Raz** Fair enough. It isn't.

**Ian** He's my friend. Except the funny thing is, we actually hadn't met face to face until the day you got me sectioned.

**Lauren** I didn't get you sectioned.

**Ian** You bloody did.

**Lauren** I just contacted medical professionals. I just told them what I'd seen.

**Ian** Bollocks.

**Raz** Ian.

**Ian** Sorry.

**Raz** Till that day we'd only talked through the door. But he was out in the garden watering.

**Ian** Heatwave.

**Raz** Yes. And I was knocking, and then I thought, well I'll put a note and leave the bags round the back in the garden. So it was only an accident we met.

**Ian** I'd have never opened the door to him. Funny, that. Like Jesus.

**Raz** Why?

**Ian** He can only knock. You have to let him in.

**Lauren** I feel like this is a prank or something. Like everyone else from work's gonna jump out in a minute from behind the sofa.

**Ian** I didn't know you knew him. He's all right isn't he?

**Lauren** He's standing right here, Dad.

**Ian** Do you do your act at her place?

**Raz** They've got a drag night every other Wednesday.

**Ian** She'll know you're a –

**Raz** Drag queen?

**Ian** Careful she don't section you.

**Lauren** Dad!

**Ian** Life in your hands wearing a dress around her.

**Lauren** You've clearly been getting on then.

**Ian** House on fire.

**Raz** We've met a couple of times.

**Lauren** But you'd talked before that.

**Ian** Yeah, through the letter box. I tell him what to get me, don't I. He tells me what he hasn't got. He never gets me eye drops.

**Lauren** Why do you need eye drops?

**Ian** It doesn't matter.

**Lauren** You never mention eye drops to me.

**Ian** I think of it as Raz's special project.

**Raz** Do you?

**Ian** Imagine how fulfilled you'll feel on the day when you finally get them.

**Raz** I think you think I think more about this stuff than I do, you know.

**Lauren** So why did you want him here today, Dad? Is he here cos you're scared of me?

**Raz** You did get him sectioned.

**Ian** I thought it could be good to have some mediation.

**Lauren** And Raz is the best person for that?

**Ian** Who else? Itchy Dave? Joe Fingers? They're useless as me.

**Raz** You're not useless, Ian.

**Ian** They don't know how to talk about feelings. Raz is good at that.

**Lauren** What feelings do you talk about with him?

**Ian** We've just had a few good conversations. And he's neighbourly. Itchy Dave isn't. Itchy Dave flashed a woman.

**Lauren** I thought you told me that didn't happen.

**Ian** It did happen, I was protecting him. Kath would have never let me see him again if she'd known he was a flasher.

**Lauren** I wish I'd known. I'd have chopped his bloody knob off.

**Raz** Let's not drift off topic, shall we?

**Ian** There, you see? He'll keep us focused.

**Lauren** This feels like you've brought along a lawyer.

**Ian** He's not a lawyer. He works in a café when he's not pole dancing down your club.

**Raz** I don't pole dance.

**Ian** He lives with his mum. He's not a lawyer.

**Raz** I can go if my being here's uncomfortable.

**Ian** Don't, Raz. He's here cos he didn't judge me. He saw me dressed the same way you did and he didn't blink. You think Joe or Dave would have done that? I wanted someone here who wasn't gonna judge me. Because I have not gone mad, you see.

**Lauren** Can I say again, this isn't fair, Dad. I didn't section you. I'm not a doctor, a doctor does that. You think I can just slip 'em a fiver? The doctor makes their mind up.

**Ian** But clearly you told them I'd gone doolally.

**Lauren** I said I was concerned because I am.

**Ian** Well *he* listened to me and *he* accepted. And he's gonna help me.

**Lauren** Help you do what?

**Ian**  This is one thing I wanted to say to you, today, Lauren. One of the reasons I've asked you here. I've thought a lot about what happened. I didn't mean for that to be a big day. But one way or another it was, and that's important. There aren't many big days left in my life. There haven't been many since your mother's funeral. So I'm gonna mark it. I'm gonna go on stage.

**Lauren**  On stage?

**Ian**  I'm gonna be a drag act. I've decided.

**Raz**  He hasn't told me this. I didn't know about this.

**Lauren**  So, what, you're gonna wear Mum's clothes in front of everyone?

**Ian**  No, I'll get my own.

**Lauren**  Is this you's done this?

**Raz**  I swear it isn't.

**Ian**  Raz can death-drop.

**Raz**  That doesn't matter.

**Ian**  But you'll help me?

**Raz**  Help you do what?

**Ian**  Well, look. Here's what I was thinking. I wondered if it could help me go outside more.

**Raz**  If you did a drag night with me?

**Ian**  That's what they say, the ones on the telly. When they do it they don't feel afraid. I thought of that, and that got me thinking. I've been afraid ever since your mum got ill. I haven't known what to do with myself. And this bloke caught me dressed like that and honestly, I was so embarrassed, but he didn't give a fuck. *You* made me feel ashamed. *You* shamed me.

**Lauren** I was shocked.

**Ian** So I want a bit of what he's got. He talked to me till I felt all right. When did I last talk to anyone like that?

**Lauren** So you want to do what he does now?

**Ian** We could do it down your club. If that's where you do it, Raz?

**Raz** If this was why you wanted me here, you could have told me mate, you know? I didn't know you were gonna say all this.

**Ian** Sorry. I'm a bit of a slow thinker. I've been working it out up here.

**Lauren** (*to Raz*) You're not here so he can talk to me. It's the other way round.

**Ian** That's not right.

**Lauren** This is about you talking to him. Aren't we sorting out us, Dad? You and me and Michael.

**Ian** You and Michael know the same thing I do. That it should have been me.

**Lauren** No one thinks that.

**Ian** Michael doesn't even visit.

**Lauren** Michael works on a rig off the coast of Aberdeen!

**Ian** He comes back now and then.

**Lauren** And when he does, he visits. Are you saying I don't visit enough? Is that what's the matter?

**Ian** Yeah, you do.

**Lauren** I never feel like you want me here.

**Ian** Course I do, love, don't be silly. It's hard to talk without your mother.

**Lauren** And you think this'll fix it?

**Ian** I thought maybe a project. I've been struggling with having no fireguard in between me and the end of life. Every day I'm just – staring at the end, like. And all the little bits spit out, and they catch me, they get in my eyes. That's not how healthy people live. Healthy people put things in between them and the fact they're going to die. Things to get on with. Things to distract them. I haven't had that for ages and ages. I think I could do with a project.

**Lauren** And this is better than model aeroplanes? Or touring the battlefields of France?

**Ian** My passport's lapsed and my hands are too shaky.

**Lauren** You know what I mean.

**Ian** I know what you mean. But look at this young man.

**Raz** Hello.

**Ian** Look at him. What if he was sent to me?

**Raz** Not really my bag, Ian.

**Lauren** I sent him, Dad. When I signed you up to the charity. For God's sake, that whole thing was me! I think I ought to go.

*Lauren stands.*

**Ian** Lauren.

**Lauren** No, it upsets me. You could have talked to me. I've been here, haven't I? I've been waiting. Would it have been so bad?

*Lauren exits.*

**Raz** Fucking hell, mate. You could have handled that better.

**Ian** Why?

43

**Raz** Oh I dunno, I'm just reading the room. Do you think this plan you've come up with is a constructive way of tackling your issues?

**Ian** Why not?

**Raz** I just think there might be higher priorities.

**Ian** Like what?

**Raz** Like her.

**Ian** All right, I get it! It's stupid and I'm thick.

**Raz** You're not thick.

**Ian** No, fuck off.

**Raz** Fucking hell. Mate, I am trying, but you are really difficult.

**Ian** I should have stopped her and given her a hug.

**Raz** Yeah, you should.

**Ian** Raz, I'm sorry.

**Raz** Fuck's sake.

**Ian** What?

**Raz** You're a fucking idiot.

**Ian** Yeah. That's always been my problem. A lot of people have said that to me.

**Raz** You've just got it jumbled up, I think. You're doing this very complex thing to fix a very simple problem.

**Ian** How is it simple?

**Raz** Well –

**Ian** How is it simple?

**Raz** All right.

**Ian** She didn't have her tea.

*Ian gets up, picks up her mug.*

You done with yours?

**Raz** Yeah.

**Ian** Give it here.

**Raz** Okay.

*Raz gives Ian his mug. Ian takes the mugs off to the kitchen. While he's offstage, Raz calls:*

If I were to help you with this, would you talk to her?

*Ian enters.*

**Ian** That's the point. To get out of myself.

**Raz** And would you shake on that? You'll try that if I help you?

**Ian** I'll shake on that.

**Raz** All right.

*They shake hands.*

I'll help you then.

**Ian** Thank you.

**Raz** I didn't know you were Lauren's dad.

**Ian** Yeah.

**Raz** She's all right. I do all right at her place.

**Ian** Think she'll let us book it?

**Raz** I dunno. I'll ask her.

**Ian** It'll be my escape. I'll need a name.

**Raz** Come again?

**Ian** A drag name.

**Raz** Oh. Yeah, I guess so.

**Ian** I was thinking of Hairy Maclary.

**Raz** That'll be under copyright.

**Ian** Can you not have names out of books?

**Raz** Not really. And you ought to make it up.

**Ian** I could be Nearly Man.

**Raz** Why?

**Ian** That's what I was.

**Raz** Not blue enough.

**Ian** No. What about Adult Mag Exchange Centre?

**Raz** Adult Mag Exchange Centre? That would be your name?

**Ian** Yeah.

**Raz** Why?

**Ian** When you get off the train in Bolton, that's almost the first thing you see. There's this sex shop with that sign above it. 'Adult Mag Exchange Centre'. And I always think, fucking hell that's depressing. That's a name for the world I come from. That's my culture. Second-hand porn. On the front door they have a sign says 'We have a more private entrance round the back if you're shy'. I always liked that. Of course, I've never been in.

**Raz** 'Adult Mag Exchange Centre'. I think it's great.

**Ian** Yeah?

**Raz** It's great.

**Ian** All right. I'll do it. I can't start without a name. That's how I always was with bands, too. Start with the name and the album cover. Never got as far as the music.

**Raz** What was the name of your band when you were growing up?

**Ian**  Living By Vice. Which was stupid, cos we didn't.

**Raz**  What sort of music?

**Ian**  Big guitar noise like a motorbike starting. I was a biker, but I ran myself over.

**Raz**  How did you do that?

**Ian**  Easy. You just fall off.

**Raz**  Well then, you'll be all right with drag.

**Ian**  Yeah?

**Raz**  I always say it's as easy as falling off a bike.

*Lights. Ian stands. He sings.*

### 4

*Ian's front room. Lauren enters with shopping. Ian is watching TV.*

**Lauren**  All right?

**Ian**  Hiya love.

**Lauren**  Got you your shopping.

**Ian**  Thanks.

**Lauren**  I'll stick it away.

**Ian**  Make us a tea will you?

**Lauren**  Sure.

*Lauren exits.*

**Ian**  *Place in the Sun* man died.

**Lauren**  *(off)* I know. Not the one I fancy though?

**Ian**  No. Still, shocking.

**Lauren**  *(off)* This pesto's off.

**Ian** What pesto?

**Lauren** (*off*) In the fridge.

**Ian** Chuck it out then. Sorry.

**Lauren** (*off*) No bother.

**Ian** How's that tea coming?

**Lauren** (*off*) Hang on!

**Ian** I dreamed your mother came back last night. Not to this house. A different house I'd never seen. It was a bit like where we used to go on holiday, back when you two were little kids. Except it wasn't by the sea. It was sort of in the middle of some mountains, and there was a long outside place for drinking coffee. Your mum was there, and at first she was happy. And then parts of her started disappearing. Her hands went, and her arms and her body. Her hair went, her laugh, her memories, her jokes. In the end she was just a mouth speaking. And I tried to grab hold of her and put her in my pocket. But she went chattering away up the stairs, and I woke up with this terrible feeling.

*Enter Lauren with tea.*

**Lauren** Sorry, did you say something?

**Ian** No, you're all right. I'm down yours tomorrow.

**Lauren** It's not mine. It's the community's.

**Ian** You're the manager.

**Lauren** On behalf of everyone.

**Ian** Well, I'm down there anyway.

**Lauren** How're you gonna get there?

**Ian** I'll get the tram.

**Lauren** Are you joking?

**Ian** What?

48

**Lauren** God's sake.

**Ian** What?

**Lauren** If you can catch the tram you can do your own shopping.

**Ian** Shopping's different. I bump into everything. I go round the wrong way. I break the trolley. Don't make me go shopping.

**Lauren** Bloody selective sort of agoraphobia.

**Ian** I thought you'd be pleased.

**Lauren** No, sorry, I am. It's just that it's sleeting down tonight. What's on telly?

**Ian** Same crap. I prefer to watch it on my laptop now.

**Lauren** What?

**Ian** You can watch old stuff on YouTube. *Hotel Inspector* from 2011. I feel more comfortable watching that. People were more bigoted, but I understood them.

**Lauren** How do you know how to do that?

**Ian** Raz showed me.

**Lauren** Oh did he now?

**Ian** He knows about all that.

**Lauren** What time you down the club tomorrow then?

**Ian** Raz said morning.

**Lauren** That's not a time.

**Ian** He'll mean eleven, won't he.

**Lauren** Why?

**Ian** He's an artist. They don't get up in the morning.

**Lauren** They do if they work in the Costa round the corner.

**Ian** Is that where he works?

49

**Lauren** Round the corner from the club, yeah.

**Ian** You'd think from the way he goes on that he ran some trendy independent place and obsessed about the perfect espresso.

**Lauren** It's all an act with him.

**Ian** Do you not like him?

**Lauren** No, he's fine. I don't know what he's doing though.

**Ian** With me?

**Lauren** Yeah.

**Ian** I reckon he's just lonely.

**Lauren** And you're the solution?

**Ian** I'm the one he found.

**Lauren** I don't think it's that, Dad. He's got mates whenever I see him.

**Ian** He might just like me.

**Lauren** Don't come crying if he nicks your life savings.

**Ian** I haven't got any life savings to nick. He paid to get my door replaced, anyway.

**Lauren** Why?

**Ian** He got the police to kick it in. Don't ask.

**Lauren** I won't. Need anything else then?

**Ian** Oh.

**Lauren** What?

**Ian** I thought we might watch something.

**Lauren** Oh.

**Ian** If you wanted.

**Lauren** I was looking forward to a bath.

**Ian**  There's a bath upstairs.

**Lauren**  I'm not gonna have a bath here.

**Ian**  Why not?

**Lauren**  I'm not at home.

**Ian**  You grew up here. Fair enough.

**Lauren**  We can watch something.

**Ian**  No, you're all right.

**Lauren**  No, come on, budge over. I've got time. There'll still be hot water in another hour, won't there.

*Ian budges over. Lauren sits down.*

What's on?

**Ian**  *Gogglebox?*

**Lauren**  Yeah, go on.

*Lauren changes the channel.*

**Ian**  Do you miss your mum?

**Lauren**  Course.

**Ian**  We don't talk about her. Hard to know what to say, maybe. Hard to be the ones left behind.

**Lauren**  You did a good job, Dad.

**Ian**  What with?

**Lauren**  Looking after her.

**Ian**  Thanks, love. You were good and all. I'm sorry I pissed you off the other day. With the hurting myself.

**Lauren**  It's all right. Just don't do that. The thing with Raz just made me feel a bit shut out.

**Ian**  I didn't know you knew him. That made it worse maybe.

**Lauren** I dunno. Maybe.

**Ian** It's harder to talk to you.

**Lauren** Why?

**Ian** If I got it wrong, then there'd be no one.

**Lauren** I'm never gonna fuck off, Dad.

**Ian** She did.

**Lauren** She didn't.

**Ian** And where's your brother? See, that's the trouble, you're the last one left. So I can't come to you with things, you're too important.

**Lauren** But that's exactly what pushes us apart.

**Ian** What?

**Lauren** You not coming to me. We're not very good at this.

**Ian** I know.

**Lauren** We could be.

**Ian** I don't know how.

**Lauren** Do you want me to travel in with you tomorrow?

**Ian** I'll be all right.

**Lauren** Will you?

**Ian** I hope so.

**Lauren** I'm in anyway in the morning. Doing the banking. So I'll see you when you get there.

**Ian** That'll be nice.

*Lights change. Raz enters in drag and performs for us to take us into the interval.*

# Act Two

*Raz and Lauren are in a working men's club.*

**Lauren** He's late.

**Raz** Only five minutes.

**Lauren** I should have gone with him.

**Raz** It's not a long way.

**Lauren** He could have got lost. Or something might have happened to him.

**Raz** No.

**Lauren** You don't know.

**Raz** No.

**Lauren** We should look for him.

**Raz** It's only been five minutes. Give it a little longer.

**Lauren** I feel so embarrassed about the whole thing.

**Raz** How do you mean?

**Lauren** Well it's embarrassing, innit? My dad doesn't go outside.

**Raz** He's just not well, there's no shame in it.

**Lauren** I just mean I should have found a way to help him.

**Raz** It's not your fault, don't worry.

**Lauren** I worry all the time.

**Raz** I can sort of tell, yeah.

**Lauren**  This could be him, look.

*Ian enters.*

All right Dad?

**Ian**  Hello love.

**Lauren**  You okay?

**Ian**  I found it a hard journey.

**Lauren**  Got here all right though?

**Ian**  Yeah, no bother.

**Lauren**  Well. That's good then.

**Ian**  Yeah, I'm happy.

**Lauren**  I won't stick around. You'll want it private.

**Ian**  Oh, yeah, sure.

**Raz**  You can stay if you want?

**Lauren**  No, it's fine.

**Ian**  You can come if we get a show together.

**Raz**  If?

**Ian**  Well this whole idea might be stupid.

**Lauren**  It's definitely stupid. That doesn't mean it won't happen.

**Ian**  No, I suppose not.

**Lauren**  I'll have to come, Dad, I'll be working the bar, won't I.

**Ian**  Yeah, I suppose so. Well then. I'll see you.

**Lauren**  All right.

**Ian**  Give us a hug then.

*They hug.*

**Lauren** (*to Raz*) Someone'll be in before too long, so you probably won't have to lock up.

**Raz** All right.

**Lauren** I'll see you later then.

**Ian** Love you.

**Lauren** Don't do anything bloody stupid.

*Lauren exits.*

**Raz** Hello mate.

**Ian** All right?

**Raz** How you doing?

**Ian** I'm okay.

**Raz** You sure?

**Ian** Little bit shaky.

**Raz** Need a sit down?

**Ian** Do you mind?

**Raz** Course not. Come on. D'you want a glass of water?

**Ian** Thank you.

**Raz** Hang on.

*Raz gets him a glass of water.*

Here you go.

*Raz gives the water to Ian, who drinks.*

**Ian** Takes it out of me, you know? Just stepping out the front door.

**Raz** Well you made it now, so good on you.

**Ian** I nearly turned back.

**Raz** Yeah?

**Ian** The tram was very busy.

**Raz** We could try and do taxis.

**Ian** I don't have the money.

**Raz** It's not that far.

**Ian** I still won't have it. I thought I was having a panic attack.

**Raz** On the tram?

**Ian** Isn't that pathetic?

**Raz** Not at all. Be easier next time.

**Ian** I had a panic attack once on a plane. Long long ago when the kids were still little. I think it was because I'd drunk too much. I woke up, we were somewhere over France, and I started shouting that they had to land, because I needed to get off. They made me lie in the aisle with my feet in the air and fed me chicken.

**Raz** Did that help?

**Ian** It did actually.

**Raz** I'll remember that then.

**Ian** In case of emergencies.

**Raz** Yeah, exactly.

**Ian** They say you shouldn't fly now. Not if you don't have to. Makes me feel terrible about those cheap trips we did.

**Raz** Don't, I'm the same. I've made a deal with myself, when I go away I'll do that by bus or whatever, by boat.

**Ian** This is your little relocation plan?

**Raz** Yeah.

**Ian** How's it going?

**Raz**  I'm getting there, actually. Getting my plan and my money.

**Ian**  Oh yeah? Where are you thinking of going?

**Raz**  I was thinking Portugal.

**Ian**  Fish. That's what they're famous for.

**Raz**  And pastel de natas.

**Ian**  One thing I'd say though.

**Raz**  Go on?

**Ian**  They don't speak Spanish. You assume they're going to, but Portuguese is different. Sounds a bit like it, but they've got their own language.

**Raz**  Thanks for that, Ian.

**Ian**  I speak from bitter experience. Our friends Rog and Jilly had a timeshare outside Lisbon and we thought we'd have a great time, cos we'd done Seville. I tell you what, we couldn't look Jilly and Rog in the eye when we got back home. Portugal is not Spain. That's all I'll say about it.

**Raz**  Well, that's good to know, thanks. Shall we make a start?

**Ian**  If we must.

**Raz**  You're hard work, aren't you.

**Ian**  Why'd you bother with me then?

**Raz**  Somehow it seems important. A lot of my mates would hate you. They want to live in a space you can't come into. I decided I'd go in a different direction. I'm going to show you and everyone like you how small you've been. How much better you could have been doing. That the world can run on kindness, and generosity, and no judgement, and love. I'm assuming you don't know your measurements?

**Ian** What for?

**Raz** What do you mean?

**Ian** What measurements?

**Raz** Well, for your body. Your chest and your waist and the like.

**Ian** Why do you need that?

**Raz** You're gonna need a dress, Ian.

**Ian** Fuck me. In at the deep end.

**Raz** I'll be quick.

**Ian** As the bishop said to the actress. Please don't tell me what any of them are.

**Raz** Okay.

**Ian** This isn't really my body, you see.

**Raz** No?

**Ian** I'm much younger and fitter than this. I'm just in disguise so I don't embarrass all the blokes who've let themselves go.

*Raz gets back up.*

So that little list of numbers is me?

**Raz** Yeah.

**Ian** And you'll go off and make an outfit out of it.

**Raz** What do you wanna look like?

**Ian** I don't know really. A man in drag.

**Raz** We can do that.

**Ian** Wonders never cease.

**Raz** Colour preference?

**Ian** Might as well be red.

**Raz** Yeah?

**Ian** Go all out.

**Raz** Why is red 'all out'?

**Ian** Chris de Burgh. Red's for romance.

**Raz** We can do red.

**Ian** What sort of music am I going to sing?

**Raz** What sort of music do you like?

**Ian** Dusty Springfield.

**Raz** Really?

**Ian** What?

**Raz** You don't strike me as her core demographic.

**Ian** I like other stuff at home. But that's what the drag acts sang when me and Kath were courting.

**Raz** Fair enough.

**Ian** What about you, what do you sing?

**Raz** Oh, anything really. Bit more modern than that maybe.

**Ian** Modern's dreadful.

**Raz** You just think that cos you're old.

**Ian** No, it is though, it's shite.

**Raz** All right, fair enough. Now I want to practise walking.

**Ian** Walking?

**Raz** Walking in high heels.

**Ian** Oh right.

**Raz** Size tens, yeah?

**Ian** That's it.

**Raz** Here you go.

**Ian** How long are these?

**Raz** Six inch heels.

**Ian** Is there not something gentler we can start with?

**Raz** This is what you get.

*Ian starts changing into them.*

**Ian** You know I never even tried this as a kid. Is it hard?

**Raz** It's not too hard. But you have to stand different.

**Ian** Different how?

**Raz** You'll see. And you have to walk with a bit of swing. Watch this.

*Raz does a twirl for Ian.*

Sassy, yeah?

**Ian** Sassy.

**Raz** That's how you have to do it.

**Ian** I don't know if I'm equal to sassy.

**Raz** Well let's have a look at you. Come on, on your feet.

*Ian stands up.*

**Ian** Ooh, bloody hell, it's different. My bum's sticking out!

**Raz** Try and straighten up a bit. There you go mate! Now, can you walk to me?

**Ian** All right.

*Ian walks towards Raz. He finds it incredibly difficult.*

Bloody hell!

**Raz** All right. But you have to swing your hips a bit.

**Ian**  Swing my hips?

**Raz**  Watch what I'm doing.

*Raz walks.*

Now can you walk to me?

*Ian walks to Raz.*

**Ian**  I feel really stupid.

**Raz**  That's because you're trying.

**Ian**  My calves hurt.

**Raz**  Try it again, go on.

**Ian**  I'm gonna do it well now.

**Raz**  Don't break your ankle.

**Ian**  I won't break my ankle. Here goes nothing.

*Ian tries again, and he's better.*

There you go, how was that?!

**Raz**  That was good mate, brilliant!

**Ian**  Shall I do it again?

**Raz**  Yeah, once more for luck.

**Ian**  Okay.

*Ian turns and walks again. But this time he falls over.*

Fuck.

**Raz**  You okay?

**Ian**  Fine.

**Raz**  Have you broken your ankle?

**Ian**  No, I don't think so.

**Raz**  I told you not to break your ankle.

**Ian** Can you help me up?

**Raz** Sure thing.

*Raz helps Ian back onto his feet.*

Told you. It's as easy as falling off a bike.

*Ian starts to laugh.*

What? What's funny?

**Ian** Oh, no, nothing. I'm just very grateful. This is just exactly what I want to be doing right now.

*Lights change. Ian sings.*

2

*Ian, Raz and Lauren come into the club.*

**Lauren** Baltic out there.

**Ian** English summer rain.

**Raz** I might get the heaters on so we can dry out.

*Raz exits.*

**Lauren** That was all right, wasn't it.

**Ian** Yeah, better this time. Thanks for coming with me.

**Lauren** Glad to. If it helps.

**Ian** I'll get back into it. It'll get easier. Funny how everything gets too much though. They say that, when you start getting older. Anything you wanna be able to do, keep doing it often cos you'll never get it back. I thought they meant touching your toes or running five K, I didn't think they meant getting on trams. I might just –

**Lauren** Oh, sure.

*Exit Ian. Enter Raz.*

**Raz**  He all right?

**Lauren**  Powdering his nose. Is he any good then?

**Raz**  He's all right, yeah.

**Lauren**  Really?

**Raz**  He's great. He stops being all tied up.

**Lauren**  How'd you mean?

**Raz**  It distracts him. So he feels better.

**Lauren**  That's good.

**Raz**  I think I'm the same.

**Lauren**  Do your family like it?

**Raz**  What, me performing? Yeah, my mum loves it. She comes down to see me all the time.

**Lauren**  She's supportive?

**Raz**  Yeah.

**Lauren**  Was she always supportive? There wasn't a time where she was. You know.

**Raz**  Not supportive?

**Lauren**  Like, when you first came out to her.

**Raz**  Yeah?

**Lauren**  Well. How did you first come out to her?

**Raz**  Oh.

**Lauren**  Is that a rude question?

**Raz**  No, it's fine. I just sat her down really. She already knew, like.

**Lauren**  Oh right.

**Raz**  I've always been who I am.

**Lauren**  Yeah. Of course. I guess that would make it easier.

**Raz**  Well, she loved me, so I knew it would be fine. Not that you don't worry. But I knew it would be fine.

*Ian enters.*

**Lauren**  All right then. I'll leave you to it.

**Ian**  I feel like a kid getting dropped off at school.

**Lauren**  Yeah, well. Shall I travel home with you?

**Ian**  No, I'll be fine now. I think I've got the hang of it.

**Lauren**  You sure?

**Ian**  I think so. I think I'll be all right.

**Lauren**  All right. Nice one. See you later. Raz.

**Raz**  See you later, Lauren.

**Lauren**  All right.

*Lauren exits.*

**Raz**  I've got something for you to try on.

**Ian**  Oh yeah?

**Raz**  You up for working on your look today?

**Ian**  Yeah, I guess so. If that's what you've got planned for us.

*Raz takes out some padding.*

What's that?

**Raz**  Padding.

**Ian**  Do I wear that?

**Raz**  Course.

**Ian** I'll need less than you. Curves in all the right places.

**Raz** Wanna try it on? I put a screen up.

**Ian** Oh, thanks.

*Ian gets changed behind the screen.*

It's a bit like football, this.

**Raz** The changing room?

**Ian** Yeah. I used to play.

**Raz** Any good?

**Ian** No.

**Raz** I played too.

**Ian** Any good?

**Raz** No.

**Ian** I liked it. Turning up with your boot bag. The smell of old mud. I was a left back. They're the worst players.

**Raz** Were you left footed?

**Ian** No, I was just the worst player.

*Ian comes out from behind the screen.*

I look like the Michelin Man.

**Raz** For now. I wanna have a go at your face.

**Ian** How'd you mean?

**Raz** Your make-up. I wanna try and find you a look. Sit down here with me.

**Ian** Oh right.

*Ian and Raz sit down opposite each other.*

**Raz** I'm just gonna fuck around and see what we like, okay?

**Ian**  Sure, yeah.

**Raz**  Nice one.

*Raz starts painting Ian's face.*

**Ian**  How did you get into this then? Was it trying on your mum's shoes like they all say on the telly?

**Raz**  A bit, yeah. And I was jealous of the girls at school.

**Ian**  What, cos they were beautiful?

**Raz**  Am I not beautiful?

**Ian**  Not like that mate.

**Raz**  I envied the make-up actually.

**Ian**  I don't care about this bit really. If drag could be anything, I wouldn't wear any. The perfect drag act I can imagine would be me, dressed as me, but not ashamed. Shouldn't I do it myself?

**Raz**  Takes practice. Lots of people do it for each other.

**Ian**  Do they?

**Raz**  Some.

**Ian**  It'll look better if you do it.

**Raz**  Once you've seen what I do you can practise yourself at home.

**Ian**  No, this is easier.

**Raz**  You ought to try. This is all part of it. It's not only the show at the end. All of this is a part of it, too.

**Ian**  Shouldn't I have made the dress, then?

**Raz**  I'm helping you with the bits that are difficult.

**Ian**  Are we trying on the dress today and all?

**Raz**  We are. It's in that bag over there. Hey, hold still.

**Ian** Sorry. I got excited.

**Raz** How would you feel about going next month?

**Ian** Going where?

**Raz** Performing.

**Ian** Really?

**Raz** I thought maybe.

**Ian** As quick as that?

**Raz** No point waiting, you'll learn when you do it.

**Ian** I'm not gonna do it more than once.

**Raz** We'll see.

**Ian** I'm not. It's just an adventure.

**Raz** We'll see.

**Ian** Do you think I'll be ready next month?

**Raz** I reckon you might be. We'll work harder if we've got a deadline. There's a night here, second Thursday. Right, this is very light, it's not a proper face. But it's something to work with. Wanna take a look?

**Ian** All right.

*Raz passes Ian a mirror and gets up, crossing to the dress.*

Look at that.

**Raz** Okay then, now for the moment of truth. It took a lot of sewing so be nice if you can, yeah?

*Raz whips out Ian's dress. It's red, and covered in feathers and sequins.*

**Ian** Fuck me, that is incredibly loud.

**Raz** It has to be loud so people hear it.

**Ian**  It'll give you tinnitus.

**Raz**  Try it on then.

**Ian**  Yeah?

**Raz**  I think you ought to.

**Ian**  Hand it over then.

*Raz holds out the dress and Ian takes it. He holds it up at first, taking it in.*

That's mad, that. This is dead exciting. It looks a bit small.

**Raz**  No, it's your size.

**Ian**  All right.

*Ian starts changing to get into it.*

I tell you, I wish Kath could see this.

**Raz**  She'd be dead chuffed, mate.

**Ian**  You think? Sorry, I'm a bit of an eyesore.

**Raz**  What do you mean?

**Ian**  Having to watch me changing.

**Raz**  Oh, babe, it's a body, it helps you get around. Don't be vain, we're all lucky to have one.

*Ian changes.*

**Ian**  Have we got a big mirror?

**Raz**  No. I can hold the small one far away.

**Ian**  Go on then.

*Raz holds up the mirror.*

Bloody hell.

*Ian struts up and down in the dress.*

**Raz**  Not bad, Ian! So you like it?

**Ian** I fucking love it, mate.

**Raz** Aw mate, I'm made up. That's great that is. Wanna photo? First time you wore the outfit?

**Ian** Yeah, go on then. Something for the scrapbook.

**Raz** I bet you have still got a scrapbook.

**Ian** Course I have.

**Raz** Bloody dinosaur you.

*Raz takes a photo.*

Go on, you can give it more than that.

*Ian strikes a pose.*

That's better!

*Raz takes another photo.*

Nice one.

**Ian** Well. This is good.

**Raz** Yeah, it is.

**Ian** What do we do now?

**Raz** Well, we could try singing?

**Ian** Yeah, great. Can we have a brew first though? I feel all – I dunno.

**Raz** It's emotional, innit.

**Ian** Yeah, I don't know why, but it is.

**Raz** Because it's gonna work! You tried and it's working.

**Ian** Yeah, I guess so.

**Raz** I'll make us both a brew then.

*Raz exits. Ian waits nervously. Raz comes back in.*

Just be a minute.

**Ian**  Yeah. I might –

**Raz**  Sure, yeah.

*Ian sits down.*

I've got a bit of news.

**Ian**  Oh yeah?

**Raz**  Bought my tickets.

**Ian**  To what?

**Raz**  To freedom. To Portugal.

**Ian**  Oh. When do you leave?

**Raz**  Once our gig's done.

**Ian**  What, that night?

**Raz**  No, no. Just a couple of days later.

**Ian**  Oh. I thought you were just talking about it.

**Raz**  No, I really want the adventure. And the sunshine.

**Ian**  Well, bloody hell. So this'll be our one gig.

**Raz**  I guess so, yeah. You did say that was what you wanted?

**Ian**  Yeah, I know.

**Raz**  We'll make it a good one.

**Ian**  Or try to.

**Raz**  You're gonna be great, Ian.

**Ian**  Yeah.

**Raz**  I'll get your tea.

*Raz exits. Raz comes back in.*

Here you go. Bag's still in.

**Ian** Ta.

**Raz** You okay?

**Ian** Yeah.

**Raz** You sure?

**Ian** I can't believe you're going.

**Raz** I'm glad we get to do this before I do.

**Ian** I'm upset if I'm honest. Sorry. Stupid. I don't know what's wrong with me.

**Raz** You're all right, mate.

**Ian** Just we've been getting on.

**Raz** Yeah, course. We can keep in touch.

**Ian** Do you reckon?

**Raz** Sure, we're mates aren't we? And I'll still be coming back to visit my mum.

**Ian** We could have a brew when you do. Sorry.

**Raz** No, it's fine. I get it.

**Ian** Yeah?

**Raz** Course I do.

**Ian** I get upset with the way everything ends, you know. In your life, sometimes you like things. You enjoy something you're doing, or you make a new friend. And I wish such things didn't end as well as start, like. I'm not very good at moving on.

**Raz** No. I see that. But you'll have Lauren.

**Ian** I think we'll be closer now I can leave the house. We could do stuff.

**Raz** Yeah, exactly.

**Ian** We could go to the Lake District.

**Raz** Whatever floats your boat, Ian.

**Ian** I used to like it out there. Lauren might go on a holiday with me.

*Ian sings.*


3

*Lauren enters and finds Ian sitting alone in the dark.*

**Lauren** All right Dad?

**Ian** Hiya.

**Lauren** You're still here.

**Ian** That's very observant.

**Lauren** You been drinking?

**Ian** A bit.

**Lauren** Hope you've paid for it.

**Ian** How could I? The bar wasn't open.

**Lauren** Well I'm here now. What have you had?

**Ian** Too much probably.

**Lauren** God's sake.

**Ian** Sorry.

**Lauren** It's all right, I'll sort it out.

**Ian** I've got money.

**Lauren** Give us your wallet?

*Ian hands his wallet over.*

I've taken for a double whisky.

**Ian** I've had more than that.

**Lauren** Let's keep it between us, shall we?

*Lauren puts the money behind the till.*

Punters'll come in soon.

**Ian** Yeah.

**Lauren** If you don't wanna see 'em.

**Ian** I'll go in a minute, don't worry.

**Lauren** What's up?

**Lauren** You've got a face like a smacked arse and you're half-cut, so what's up?

**Ian** Oh, nothing.

**Lauren** Where's Raz?

**Ian** Huh.

**Lauren** What?

**Ian** That fucking poof?

**Lauren** Excuse me?

**Ian** What?

**Lauren** You do not talk like that in here.

**Ian** He's gone home.

**Lauren** As should you.

**Ian** He's leaving.

**Lauren** What d'you mean?

**Ian** He's moving away.

**Lauren** And?

**Ian** And nothing.

**Lauren** No, not 'and nothing'.

**Ian**  All right, I was getting to like him.

**Lauren**  But you'll call him a fucking poof all the same?

**Ian**  I'm sorry.

**Lauren**  For God's sake.

**Ian**  I thought people said that now? People said they were poofs all the time, I heard.

**Lauren**  Queer, Dad. People say they're queer. Still doesn't mean you can use it like that.

**Ian**  Fuck's sake.

**Lauren**  What?

**Ian**  I get frustrated.

**Lauren**  With the nomenclature of the queer community?

**Ian**  No, with me! With never fucking getting it. I didn't mean to be offensive.

**Lauren**  You can't say 'poof' like that, it's homophobic.

**Ian**  I don't want to be homophobic.

**Lauren**  Then fucking don't be.

**Ian**  Yeah, I'm sorry. I shouldn't ever say anything.

**Lauren**  It's okay to be upset your friend's leaving. You don't have to pretend you don't feel things.

**Ian**  No, it's better. Else it comes out the wrong way. I don't give a toss if someone's gay. I really don't think it's any of my business.

**Lauren**  Shame really.

**Ian**  Why?

**Lauren**  Could be a good niche for you. 'Manchester's Only Homophobic Drag Queen'.

**Ian** Don't.

**Lauren** I'm joking.

**Ian** That's not who I want to be. I just want to be able to –
you know?

**Lauren** No, I don't, Dad, you have to use your words.

**Ian** Don't be on at me.

**Lauren** I'm not being on at you!

**Ian** I wanna be like the old me.

**Lauren** You will be. Give it time. Time's all that's needed.

**Ian** No.

**Lauren** Why not?

**Ian** Time's the fucking enemy. You know what I realised
while I was drinking? Raz doesn't matter. Doesn't matter
if he's leaving. He's turned up so late in my story, and he's
gonna piss off out of it so quickly, few years from now he'll
barely merit a mention. That's most people, they come and
they go. But time. That is always there. Taking things away
from you.

**Lauren** Will you help me with the chairs?

**Ian** All right.

*They take chairs off tables.*

Like your mum aren't you.

**Lauren** Am I?

**Ian** Just the same.

**Lauren** How so?

**Ian** Every Saturday morning. 'Can you get this driveway
cleaned?' 'Can you get these shelves on the wall please?'
'When are you going to water the garden?'

75

**Lauren** Jesus, I only asked for a hand.

**Ian** No, I like it. I liked feeling useful. I was always good for getting things from high places. I might need to sit down again.

**Lauren** How much have you had?

**Ian** Most of a bottle.

**Lauren** Dad!

**Ian** Do you know what it's like on your own?

**Lauren** For fuck's sake, grow up! Why d'you think you're the only one suffering? Didn't I lose my mum as well? Do you think no one else ever lost anyone? Everyone who drinks in this club is probably dealing with something.

**Ian** I know that. I'm just fucking sad, aren't I. I don't want you to think I'm a homophobe.

**Lauren** It's fine, Dad.

**Ian** No, it isn't. Raz doesn't matter, but you do, Lauren. You are one of my longest relationships. I have known you your whole life.

**Lauren** Well you're my dad, aren't you.

**Ian** Exactly. As far as either of us know. So believe me when I tell you I know things about you.

**Lauren** Like what?

**Ian** I've changed your bloody nappies.

**Lauren** Give it a few years I'll be returning the favour.

**Ian** Oh, no. You don't think that, do you? You don't think that'll happen?

**Lauren** It's all right, you've got a while yet. I'm gonna call you a cab.

**Ian** I'm fine.

**Lauren** No, you need to go home to bed.

**Ian** But you've had my spending money for the whisky.

**Lauren** Cab's on me. You'll get lost on the tram.

**Ian** I'll be sick on the tram.

**Lauren** Exactly.

**Ian** Do you think there's any chance Raz won't go?

**Lauren** I don't think so, Dad. He's handed in his notice at the café.

**Ian** Shame. I thought we might get a regular thing going.

**Lauren** Yeah?

**Ian** If we went down well the first time. Here, Lauren, look at this.

*Ian waltzes with a chair.*

Not bad, eh?

**Lauren** Cab's two minutes away.

**Ian** How do you know?

**Lauren** They show you on your phone.

**Ian** Let's see?

**Lauren** Seriously?

**Ian** Yeah, come on, show me.

**Lauren** It's just a map but they show you where they are.

**Ian** He's facing in the wrong direction.

**Lauren** Don't pay too much attention to that.

**Ian** Oh, he's turned round, look.

**Lauren** Yeah.

**Ian** That's good.

*Lights change. Raz sings.*


4


*Ian is rehearsing onstage. He gets his steps wrong. Raz is watching.*

**Ian** Fuck it.

**Raz** Don't worry. Let's do it again.

**Ian** All right.

*Ian tries again.*

Better.

**Raz** Getting there.

**Ian** But not right?

**Raz** You'll get it, Ian. Repetition repetition repetition.

**Ian** Repetition.

**Raz** Repetition.

**Ian** Repetition repetition repetition –

*Raz joins in.*

**Both** – repetition repetition repetition!

**Ian** Tell you what.

**Raz** What?

**Ian** Have you ever done something.

**Raz** How do you mean?

**Ian** Hang on, I hadn't finished. Have you ever done something that's actually good? I don't mean doing it all right. I mean, like, world class. Best in the world at it.

**Raz** God, no way.

**Ian** I don't think I ever will in my life. I feel very envious of people who find that.

**Raz** But who does? Simone Biles? It's quite rare, innit.

**Ian** Unless.

**Raz** What?

**Ian** Well, when you think about it. Maybe I was the best husband Kath ever had. Maybe I was the world's best father to Lauren. I mean, not literally, I was a hopeless dad.

**Raz** No you weren't.

**Ian** I could have been better. I just mean – I was the only one she had. Have you got brothers?

**Raz** No.

**Ian** Then you're the world's best son to your parents. We can be best in the world at that.

**Raz** At what?

**Ian** Family. How many more rehearsals do we have?

**Raz** Well, I thought we could run it through Wednesday.

**Ian** And that's it?

**Raz** I think so.

**Ian** As quick as that? I'm not ready.

**Raz** You are.

**Ian** I can't do it. What if this cold gets worse and I can't go on?

**Raz**  It's not a cold, you've just strained your top register. Have a lemon and ginger before you go to bed.

**Ian**  And honey.

**Raz**  Yeah.

**Ian**  Honey's good for the throat. We've never done the whole thing straight through.

**Raz**  I know.

**Ian**  We've only done it spit spat spot.

**Raz**  That's why I thought we could run it on Wednesday.

**Ian**  I don't think I'll be able to do it.

**Raz**  Ian, don't worry. We all feel this way. People always feel like they need more rehearsal.

**Ian**  It's not that.

**Raz**  What then?

**Ian**  I don't want it to finish.

**Raz**  Oh, you'll have to take that up with whichever God you pray to, Ian, I can't help you with that.

*Lights change. Ian sings.*

## 5

*Lights change and we're backstage before the show. Lauren and Raz. Lauren is holding a stack of chairs.*

**Lauren** Is Dad –

**Raz** He's just changing.

**Lauren** He all right?

**Raz** He's nervous.

**Lauren** I would be and all. But you got it out of him. It's really good of you, I'm grateful.

**Raz** I've enjoyed it.

**Lauren** If this was a film, you and me might fall in love now.

**Raz** Yeah. But you're not really my type, love.

**Lauren** You're not mine either.

**Raz** Oh. I didn't realise.

**Lauren** I've been a bit slow doing anything about it. I always felt ashamed, you know? My mum was a terror. He won't tell you. But if she said it was snowing, it was snowing, know what I mean? So I pushed myself very deep down. Any part of me that might not seem tidy. Cos I got in such trouble if the cushions weren't straight.

**Raz** Way Ian talks about her you'd think she was Mother Teresa.

**Lauren** I know. It's hard, that. If he'd stop pretending she was perfect, it might be easier.

**Raz** Does he know about this?

**Lauren** No. Don't tell him.

**Raz** What are you scared of?

**Lauren**  Being untidy.

**Raz**  Fuck that. Make a mess. Make all the mess you like.

**Lauren**  Yeah. I think I'd like to. I've never done that.

*Ian enters.*

All right, Dad.

**Ian**  You two all right?

**Raz**  I'm gonna go and treat myself to a tequila.

**Ian**  Everything okay?

**Raz**  Yeah. Pre-match ritual. See you in a minute.

*Raz exits.*

**Ian**  You okay?

**Lauren**  Yeah, just saying hi.

**Ian**  Oh. Hi! Good with people, that lad, isn't he. Gets us talking.

**Lauren**  Yeah.

**Ian**  What you doing back here?

**Lauren**  We needed more chairs. You know all your old men are in?

**Ian**  I asked 'em.

**Lauren**  Reckon they'll like it?

**Ian**  They bloody should. They're bloody lucky to be entertained by me.

**Lauren**  I'll film it for Michael.

**Ian**  Would you? I'd love that.

**Lauren**  He'll like it. I forgot you could sing.

**Ian**  You joking? I sang all the time.

**Lauren** When we were young maybe. Not when we were older.

**Ian** Could you help me do this up?

**Lauren** Sure, yeah.

*Lauren does up Ian's dress.*

**Ian** For a little while back there I wasn't a person. Now I'm here in a working men's club, and there's a pint waiting for me on the bar when I've done this. And I can handle that. I'm looking forward to it. Funny what gets you back in the swing. How do I look?

*Ian does a twirl.*

**Lauren** Great, yeah.

**Ian** We could have a proper catch-up once this is over.

**Lauren** That'd be nice, yeah.

**Ian** You don't hate me?

**Lauren** Course I don't hate you Dad, don't be stupid.

**Ian** Cos I was thinking if you wanted we could go on holiday.

**Lauren** That might be nice. We'll talk after, maybe.

**Ian** Yeah, all right. We'll talk when it's done.

*Enter Raz.*

**Raz** All right you two? Feeling excited?

**Ian** Shitting myself, mate.

**Raz** Hopefully not literally.

**Ian** Lauren and I are going on holiday!

**Raz** Good. That's lovely.

**Ian** We don't know where we're going.

**Lauren** We could think about that later maybe.

**Ian** Yeah. I was thinking the Lake District, where we used to go when you were at school? Or we could go to Portugal and visit Raz.

**Raz** Don't do that.

**Ian** Oh.

**Raz** I don't mean to be rude. But if you're gonna do something, make it about you two. I grew up without my dad. He died. I needed my mother. Don't visit me, look after each other.

**Ian** Yeah. Sorry, Raz, I didn't know you lost your dad.

**Raz** I didn't lose him, he died, he's not a wallet.

**Ian** All right. You know what I mean.

**Raz** Yeah. I don't remember much about him, except he was scary.

**Ian** I was pretty scared of Lauren's mum, if I'm honest. But you love them all the same.

**Lauren** Do you guys need to do a warm-up?

**Ian** Fuck that, we'll be fine.

**Raz** Ever the professional. Come on, treat it serious. Everyone you know's out there.

**Ian** This is fucking awful, but I like it.

**Lauren** I'd better get these back.

**Ian** All right. Love you.

**Lauren** Love you. See you later.

*Lauren exits with the chairs.*

**Raz** So this is it.

**Ian**  Yeah. Listen, Raz –

**Raz**  Yeah?

**Ian**  I'm so grateful.

**Raz**  Yeah. Well. We got here, didn't we. Now we just have to actually do it.

**Ian**  I could do with one more piss.

**Raz**  Too late. Come on, scales!

*Ian sings a scale.*

Again.

*Ian sings a higher one.*

And one for luck!

*Ian sings a final scale.*

Nice one. Right, I'll go and warm 'em up.

**Ian**  Serious?

**Raz**  Yeah, it's time, Ian.

**Ian**  Bloody hell.

**Raz**  I'll see you out there. Come on when I call your name.

**Ian**  All right. See you out there.

**Raz**  Break a leg!

*Raz exits.*

**Ian**  Thank you.

*Ian listens for a moment.*

Oh, I've gone and done it now, love. Here's another fine mess I've got into.

*Lights change. They are onstage together.*

**Raz** A round of applause for my best girlfriend, Adult Mag Exchange Centre!

**Ian** Thank you, everyone, thank you very much.

**Raz** Let me tell you a bit about this one. Two months ago she was under a rock. She'd gone half mad from years indoors with just her and her internet service provider. Half blind, terrible RSI, the usual. But our Lauren at the back there, hello Lauren, she let us have the stage for tonight to shake off some cobwebs, and here she is before you! A new woman! A woman without any shame!

**Ian** What can I say, it's true, I'm shameless.

**Raz** Adult Mag Exchange Centre and I were put together by a charity called Helping Hands.

**Ian** She knows all about that.

**Raz** Helping Hands set us up and we're glad that happened, cos Adult Mag Exchange Centre hadn't seen people since the passing of Kath. Lauren's mother. Who I believe used to come here and who I know is missed. So what we'd like to do now, if you'll allow us, is me and her, we're gonna propose a toast. Charge your glasses, everyone, thank you. And raise 'em now to remember a good woman. Kath, I never knew you. But I know your family. And they're fucking exhausting, so you must have been a saint. No, but seriously, they are awful people. But don't take my word for it. You can hear for yourself. Ladies and gentlemen, Adult Mag Exchange Centre!

**Ian** Thank you! Thank you very much.

*Ian drains his drink. He starts to sing. After a short while, he breaks into speech.*

I loved you. We were just leaving school. I'd always loved you. You'd never known who I was till then. But sometimes, a night comes when you get a chance. You have to take it.

A club like this one. Smoke and lights and music. You looked at me and I thought, I've pulled. At the end of the night you took my hand. You asked me, 'Where are we going to now, love?'

I loved you. When we bought our first home. Newly married, inventing the world. We got a sofa on hire purchase. A double bed. A television.

I loved you. When we first brought Michael home, and I quit smoking, because the world was different. I wanted a long time with my children. I wanted a long time with you. We put up that mobile, we used to read to him. Then we were the same with Lauren. Every time we fought or got tired of each other, I loved you. Every vanished dream.

I loved you from the moment you chose me. And that saved me. When I got scared about money, or having to find a job again, I always managed, no matter how hard things got. Because I'd been loved and saved by you. Because you were so much better than I were.

I loved you. When you first started complaining. And said you had no energy now. I loved you when we went to the doctor. I loved you when you started having to wear a wig. I loved you when you were four stone lighter. And when you used to just sit in the chair, and look out the window at the back garden, and tell me that I had to keep it tidy, and whatever happened I had to keep going, or from beyond the grave you'd never forgive me.

I loved you when they said it was over. Every last day I held your hand. In the living room, in the hospice. Every day I was saved by you. So this is my song for you, my darling. Offered in tribute to the place where it began. In the stink and the smoke of a club like this one, long gone, like you, long time vanished. Here again for one night only. That night you first took my hand.

*Ian sings.*

*End.*